Presented to

*Dylan Engels*

by *Grandma Betty*

on *Christmas 2003*

# I'm Jack!

## I AM MADE TO RUN AND PLAY

Crystal Bowman
Illustrated by Elena Kucharik

Tyndale House Publishers, Inc.
WHEATON, ILLINOIS

Visit Tyndale's exciting Web site at www.tyndale.com

Edited by Betty Free Swanberg
Designed by Catherine Bergstrom

Scripture quotation is taken from the Holy Bible, New Living Translation, copyright © 1996.
Used by permission of Tyndale House Publishers, Inc., Wheaton, Illinois 60189. All rights
reserved.

**Library of Congress Cataloging-in-Publication Data**
Bowman, Crystal.
    I'm Jack! : I am made to run and play / Crystal Bowman ; illustrated by Elena Kucharik.
        p. cm. — (Little blessings)
Summary: In rhyming text, Jack describes all the ways that God gave him to move around,
from running and swimming to building and climbing.
    ISBN 0-8423-7672-0 (alk. paper)
    1. Movement, Psychology of—Religious aspects—Christianity—Juvenile literature. 2.
Exercise—Religious aspects—Christianity—Juvenile literature. [1. Play. 2. Exercise. 3. Christian
life.] I. Kucharik, Elena, ill. II. Title. III. Series. Little blessings picture books.

BV4598 .B69 2003
242'.62—dc21                                                    2002015176

Printed in Italy

09 08 07 06 05 04 03
7   6   5   4   3   2   1

To Dad:
May God give you the strength
to keep moving!

I can do everything with the
help of Christ who gives me
the strength I need.

PHILIPPIANS 4:13

2

Wiggle, wiggle,
  little toes,
Stretch my arms
  and rub my nose.
All day long
  my body grows.
      *God made me to move.*

3

4

My name's Jack.
   It's time to eat.
*Pitter, patter*
   *go my feet.*
Pour the syrup
   thick and sweet.
      *God made me to move.*

Who's that knocking
    at my door?
One friend, two friends,
    three friends, four.
Rumble, tumble
    'cross the floor.
        *God made me to move.*

7

8

Build a tower
   to the sky
Stretching up
   and reaching high.
Knock it down,
   oh me, oh my!
      *God made me to move.*

9

Racing, chasing
in the sun,

Tagging playmates
one by one.
Can't catch me—
I'm on the run!
*God made me to move.*

Swinging up
   and swinging down,
Slipping, sliding
   to the ground.

12

Whirling, twirling
round and round.
*God made me to move.*

13

Puppy wants
   to run and play;
Kick my football
   far away.
Run and fetch it—
   don't delay.
      *God made me to move.*

Splishing, splashing
in the sea,
Friends are happy
as can be!
Floating, sinking,
eyelids blinking.
*God made me to move.*

"Hello, turtle!
  Why so slow?
Follow me;
  let's go, go, go."
Everybody
  needs to know
    *God made me to move.*

"Little birdie
   in the sky,
Can you teach me
   how to fly?
Flap my arms—
   hey, watch me try!"
      *God made me to move.*

*Zoom, zoom!* Dump truck
in the sand,
Making mountains
tall and grand.
Building, smashing,
crumbling, crashing!
*God made me to move.*

Climbing higher
　up the tree.
"Uh-oh, Jack,
　you bumped your knee!"
"I'm all right—
　hey, look and see."
　　*God made me to move.*

Pass the cookies—
time to share.
Chocolate crumbs
are everywhere—

On my cheeks
   and in my hair!
      *God made me to move.*

Holding hands
   to cross the street,
Saying hi
   to friends we meet.

Skipping, walking,
laughing, talking.
*God made me to move.*

29

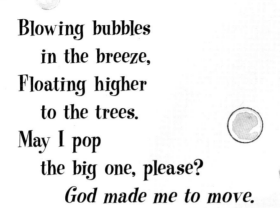

Blowing bubbles
    in the breeze,
Floating higher
    to the trees.
May I pop
    the big one, please?
        *God made me to move.*

30

31

Turn the jump rope
 round and round.
Right foot, left foot,
 up and down.
One, two, three, four,
 touch the ground.
    *God made me to move.*

33

Come and join
the marching band.
Stomp your feet
and wave your hand.

Music playing,
  swinging, swaying.
    *God made me to move.*

"Good-bye, friends,
  our day is done.
Sure has been
  a lot of fun!
Time for dinner—
  gotta run."
    *God made me to move.*

Lord, you made us
   big and small.
Fish can swim,
   and bugs can crawl.
Birds can fly
   above it all.
      *YOU made US to move.*

You made me
    from toes to chin.
Thank you for
    my bones and skin

So I can run
and jump and play,
And praise you, God,
both night and day.
*YOU made ME to move!*

41

## About the Author

Crystal Bowman received a bachelor of arts degree in elementary education from Calvin College and studied early childhood development at the University of Michigan. A former preschool teacher, she loves writing for young children and is the author of numerous children's books. Crystal is a writer and speaker for MOPS International and has written several books in the recently published MOPS picture-book series.

Besides writing books, Crystal enjoys being active in the local schools, speaking at authors' assemblies, and conducting poetry workshops. Her books of humorous poetry are favorites in the classroom as well as at literacy conferences.

Crystal is also involved in women's ministries, writing Bible study materials for her church and speaking at women's conferences. She has been a guest on many Christian radio programs and has written a book of meditations for moms.

Crystal and her husband live in Grand Rapids, Michigan, and have three grown children.

# About the Illustrator

Elena Kucharik, well-known Care Bears artist, has created the Little Blessings characters, which appear in a line of Little Blessings products for young children and their families.

Born in Cleveland, Ohio, Elena received a bachelor of fine arts degree in commercial art at Kent State University. After graduation she worked as a greeting card artist and art director at American Greetings Corporation in Cleveland.

For the past 25 years Elena has been a freelance illustrator. During this time she was the lead artist and developer of Care Bears, as well as a designer and illustrator for major corporations and publishers. For the last 10 years Elena has been focusing her talents on illustrations for children's books.

Elena and her husband live in Madison, Connecticut, and have two grown daughters.

## Products in the Little Blessings line

Bible for Little Hearts
Prayers for Little Hearts
Promises for Little Hearts
Lullabies for Little Hearts
Lullabies Cassette

Blessings Everywhere
Rain or Shine
God Makes Nighttime Too
Birthday Blessings
Christmas Blessings
God Loves You
Thank You, God!
ABC's
Count Your Blessings
Blessings Come in Shapes
Many-Colored Blessings

What Is God Like?
Who Is Jesus?
What about Heaven?
Are Angels Real?
What Is Prayer?

I'm Kaitlyn!
I'm Zoë!
I'm Jack!
I'm Parker!

Little Blessings New Testament
    & Psalms

Blessings Every Day
Questions from Little Hearts

God Created Me!
    A memory book of baby's first year